# Treasure trouble is brewing.

"My turn!" Bess declared. "My clue is totally bodacious. Go and look under the bushes."

"Bess!" George wailed as the twins ran off. "That wasn't a clue—you told them exactly where it was!"

"I didn't say *which* bush!" Bess insisted.

The girls caught up with the twins. Damien was kneeling next to the bushes, his hand stretched underneath.

"There's nothing here," Damien reported.

"Huh?" Nancy said, surprised. "It has to be there."

"Let me look," George said. Dropping to her knees she practically crawled underneath the bushes.

"What do you see, George?" Nancy asked.

"Just dirt and a bunch of pebbles," George said. She looked up with wide eyes. "The treasure chest is *gone*!"

# Join the CLUE CREW
## & solve these other cases!

# NANCY DREW

## #20 AND THE CLUE CREW

## Treasure Trouble

### BY CAROLYN KEENE

### ILLUSTRATED BY MACKY PAMINTUAN

Aladdin Paperbacks
New York London Toronto Sydney

🐦 ALADDIN PAPERBACKS

An imprint of Simon & Schuster Children's Publishing Division

1230 Avenue of the Americas, New York, NY 10020

Text copyright © 2009 by Simon & Schuster, Inc.

Illustrations copyright © 2009 by Macky Pamintuan

All rights reserved, including the right of reproduction in whole or in part in any form.

NANCY DREW, ALADDIN PAPERBACKS, and related logos are registered trademarks of Simon & Schuster, Inc.

NANCY DREW AND THE CLUE CREW is a registered trademark of Simon & Schuster, Inc.

Designed by Lisa Vega

The text of this book was set in ITC Stone Informal.

Manufactured in the United States of America

First Aladdin Paperbacks edition May 2009

10 9 8 7 6 5

Library of Congress Control Number 2008932981

ISBN: 978-1-4169-7809-1

0412 OFF

# CONTENTS

# CHAPTER ONE

## Beaches and Scream

"Stop the van!" Bess Marvin cried. "I forgot something important!"

Eight-year-old Nancy Drew turned to her best friend Bess. So did her other best friend, George Fayne.

"What did you forget?" Nancy Drew asked. "Your new swimsuit with the polka dots? Your sunglasses?"

"Those funny-looking flip-flops of yours that look like banana peels?" George asked.

All three friends were sitting side by side in the backseat of Mrs. Fayne's catering van.

"They're not funny looking!" Bess said. Her blond hair whipped Nancy's face as she shook

1

her head. "I forgot to put sunscreen between my toes. My bag is in the trunk."

George heaved a big sigh. She was Bess's cousin but with her dark hair and brown eyes looked nothing like Bess.

"You already put tons of sunscreen on, Bess," George said. "My mom's van smells like the inside of a coconut!"

Nancy took a whiff. The inside of Mrs. Fayne's van usually smelled like coleslaw and pickles. That's because cooking and delivering food was part of her catering job.

"Don't worry, Bess," Mrs. Fayne said. Her eyes twinkled in the rearview mirror as she drove. "As soon as we get to Barnacle Beach you can put on more sunscreen."

"Beach!" Nancy repeated. She was so excited, she had the wiggles. It was Tuesday morning and the start of summer vacation. The girls couldn't wait to get to Barnacle Beach to help Mrs. Fayne with a special pirate-themed party. There would be swashbuckling games, pirate decorations, a treasure chest filled with party favors—and kids, kids, kids!

"Who is the party for, Aunt Louise?" Bess asked.

"It's for twins named Ivy and Damien Teasdale," Mrs. Fayne explained. "They and their little cousin are spending the summer with their grandmother."

"Their *rich* grandmother," George added. "I heard she lives in a mansion with her own private beach."

"A private beach?" Bess said, her blue eyes flashing. "I'll bet every kid around will be at that party."

"I'm afraid not, Bess," Mrs. Fayne said. "Mrs. Teasdale sent out invitations, but no one is coming."

"Why not?" Nancy asked with surprise.

"Mrs. Teasdale didn't tell me," Mrs. Fayne said, shrugging her shoulders as she drove. "I guess it's a mystery."

If anyone knew about mysteries, it was Nancy,

Bess, and George. They had their own detective club called the Clue Crew.

"It's a mystery, all right," Bess said. "Whoever heard of a kids party without kids?"

"That's why you girls are coming," Mrs. Fayne explained. "I promised Mrs. Teasdale food, fun, and *friends*!"

The girls high-fived. Then they gazed out the car windows for signs of Barnacle Beach. The first one they saw was a colorful billboard that read WELCOME TO BARNACLE BEACH—HOME OF LONNY THE LAKE LIZARD!

"Who's Lonny the Lake Lizard?" Nancy wondered.

"You mean *what*'s Lonny the Lake Lizard?" George asked.

Mrs. Fayne drove another five minutes before pulling up to a big white house with red shutters. A sign over the front door read BARNACLE BETTY'S LAKESIDE LODGE.

"Welcome to our hotel," Mrs. Fayne announced.

"It's right up the road from the Teasdale mansion."

The girls glanced up the road to see a huge pink house. Super huge. The front yard had a rose garden and hedges trimmed to look like seahorses and dolphins.

"Not too shabby!" George exclaimed.

While Mrs. Fayne parked the van the girls carried their gear into the hotel. Nancy wheeled her purple suitcase, George carried her backpack and her mom's laptop computer case, and Bess wheeled two suitcases—one with each hand!

"What's in those suitcases, Bess?" George asked. "We're here only two days!"

"I couldn't decide which of my summer clothes to bring," Bess said with a grin. "So I brought them all!"

Once inside the hotel the girls gazed around the lobby. In the middle stood a table shaped like the steering wheel of a ship. The colorful wallpaper was decorated with a seahorse and fish design.

"I hope the hotel is near the beach," Nancy said.

"I hope it has Wi-Fi," George added, lifting the computer case. She was a computer geek—even on vacation!

A woman with short brown hair waved to them from behind the reception desk. "I'm Barnacle Betty," she said cheerily. "And I'll bet you kids are here to see Lonny the Lake Lizard!"

"Is there really a lake lizard here?" Bess asked.

"Would I be selling these if there wasn't?" Betty asked. She pulled a cap and T-shirt from under the desk. They both read I SAW LONNY AT BARNACLE BEACH!

"Did *you* ever see Lonny?" Nancy asked.

"Other people told me they did," Betty admitted. She pointed to a bunch of framed pictures hanging behind the desk. "See for yourself."

The girls leaned over the desk to get a closer

look. Most of the pictures showed a shadowy figure on the beach or in the water. He looked like some kind of giant lizard!

"Oh, no!" Bess said. "How can we go swimming with a giant lizard monster in the water?"

"Don't you worry, Goldilocks," Betty said, and laughed. "I heard Lonny is as gentle as a scaly pussycat. Just keep an eye on your beach toys and snack foods."

"How come?" Nancy asked in a hushed voice.

"Because," Betty said, leaning over the desk, "whatever Lonny the Lake Lizard wants, Lonny takes!"

Mrs. Fayne stepped up to the desk to check in. While she spoke to Betty the girls huddled together, whispering.

"Maybe we should have stayed in River Heights!" George said. "The only monsters there are my brothers."

"I hate monsters!" Bess whimpered. "More than I hate string beans, snakes, and upside-down rides."

"We never saw a monster yet, Bess," Nancy said firmly. "And we never will."

Once Mrs. Fayne had the keys they headed down the hallway to their rooms. Mrs. Fayne had her own room. Connected by a door was another, bigger room shared by the girls. It had three beds and a shell-shaped sink in the bathroom. But the best part was right outside the window.

"The beach!" Nancy exclaimed.

The three friends gazed out the window at Barnacle Beach. Grown-ups lay on beach towels while kids played in the sand and splashed in the lake. Sailboats and rowboats drifted in the distance.

"It's awesome!" Nancy gasped.

"And not a monster in sight," Bess said with relief.

"Time to get ready, girls!" Mrs. Fayne called.

Nancy, Bess, and George didn't change into their swimsuits. Instead they tied pirate bandannas around their heads and slipped beaded necklaces around their necks. Bess squirted on more sunscreen. They had a party to work on!

It wasn't long before Mrs. Fayne and the girls were unloading food and party supplies at the Teasdale mansion.

"Just bring everything into the entrance hall, please," a silver-haired woman called from the front door.

"That must be Mrs. Teasdale," Nancy said as they lugged boxes and plastic bags toward the house.

"If Mrs. Teasdale is so rich," Bess whispered, "where are the butlers and maids to help us?"

Nancy didn't see any butlers or maids, just a boy and a girl waiting in the entrance hall.

"This is Damien and Ivy." Mrs. Teasdale introduced them with a smile. "They're turning eight today."

"We're eight too," Bess said. "We're in the third grade at River Heights Elementary School."

"Ivy and Damien attend the Worthington Academy for Exceptional Children," Mrs.

Teasdale said. "It has two Olympic-sized swimming pools and a string of polo ponies."

"Our school has a frozen-yogurt machine in the lunchroom," George bragged. "It spits out sprinkles."

Damien frowned at the girls. "I thought a boy named George was supposed to come," he said.

"She's George," Bess said, pointing to her cousin. "Her real name is Georgia, but she hates it, so it's a secret."

"Until now," George snapped at Bess.

"Great," Damien mumbled to himself. "My sister, my bratty cousin Poppy, and now three more girls!"

"Where is Poppy, anyway?" Ivy asked, looking around.

"Probably getting into trouble again," Mrs. Teasdale said in a frosty voice.

Ivy and Damien went upstairs to change into pirate costumes. Nancy, Bess, and George helped Mrs. Fayne decorate the Teasdales' private beach for the party.

After tying balloons to a picnic table they looked for a good place to hide the treasure chest. Nancy saw a patch of bushes in the back of the beach.

"There!" Nancy said. "The bushes will totally cover the treasure chest."

The girls filled the chest with sparkly eye patches, plastic beads, and toy telescopes. They were about to shut the chest when—"It's not fair!" a voice screamed.

The girls whirled around. Behind them stood a girl wearing denim shorts and a stained pink T-shirt. She looked about six years old. Nancy guessed it was Poppy.

"My cousins always have cool parties!" Poppy screamed. "All I got for my birthday was lunch at Chucky Chicken!"

Bess pointed to Poppy's T-shirt and said, "Is that where you got all those stains?"

"Some of them," Poppy answered. She pointed to her stains one by one. "This is mustard from a Cubs game hot dog. This one is chocolate ice cream from the circus. . . ."

Poppy suddenly pointed at the lake. "Look!" she screamed again. "There's Lonny the Lake Monster!"

"Where? Where?" the girls said, spinning around.

"Kidding!" Poppy laughed. She kept laughing as she walked away.

"She saw us hiding the treasure chest," George said. "Should we find another place to hide it?"

"Too late!" Nancy said. "Here come Ivy and Damien!"

The girls shoved the chest under the bushes until it was totally covered by leaves and branches. Then they raced to the twins on the beach.

"Look! Pirates!" Ivy said, pointing to the lake.

"Not another joke," George grumbled.

But as the girls turned toward the lake their jaws dropped. Drifting on the water was a boat flying a black pirate flag. As Nancy looked closer she gasped. Inside the boat were two real-live pirates.

# ChaPTER TWo

## Yo, Ho, Oh, No!

"Ahoy, landlubbers!" the bigger pirate shouted. "Captain Corky and First Mate Casey at yer service!"

A parrot flapped its wings from Captain Corky's shoulders. "At yer service, at yer service!" it squawked.

Nancy shaded her eyes from the sun. She watched as Captain Corky and Casey tied their boat to the Teasdales' dock. Captain Corky was dressed in a black pirate's hat, a white shirt, and britches. An eye patch covered one eye. Casey wore a white shirt and britches too, but instead of a black hat he wore a red bandanna on his head.

The big and little pirates walked up the beach. They dragged canvas sacks behind them.

"Casey's a kid like us," George pointed out.

"He's still a pirate!" Ivy exclaimed. She pulled out a bright pink cell phone. "I'm calling Grandmother."

Damien pulled a bright blue cell phone from his pocket. "Me too," he said.

"Wait, kids," Mrs. Fayne said, running over. "I invited Captain Corky and Casey. What's a pirate party without pirates, right?"

"A boy at my party—at last!" Damien cheered.

The parrot stretched his feathery neck and squawked, "Party on! Party on! Raaaak!"

"Crackers thar is right," Captain Corky growled. "Let's get this party staaaaaaarted."

Casey and the Captain pulled a bunch of spongy toy swords out of a sack.

"But first, if you want to be buccaneers," Captain Corky said, "you have to learn a little swashbuckling!"

Everyone tried to knock the spongy swords out of each other's hands. Everyone but Poppy, that is. Nancy saw her on the beach talking quietly to Crackers perched on her hand.

*Why isn't she playing?* Nancy wondered. Her thoughts were interrupted as her sword was knocked out of her hand.

"Snooze—you lose!" George joked. She held the last sword so she was the winner.

"Fair winds, matey!" Casey told George. "Now you're a real pirate like me!"

"You're a party pirate, Casey," Damien scoffed. "Nobody's a real pirate until they find buried treasure."

"Nuh-uh!" Casey said.

"Uh-*huh*!" Damien insisted.

"That reminds me, Nancy," Bess whispered. "I'd better check on our treasure chest to make sure it's still there."

Bess ran off just as Crackers fluttered over. He landed on Nancy's shoulder and squawked loudly, "This party stinks! This party stinks! Arrrk!"

Nancy gulped as all eyes turned to her. "He said it," she blurted, nodding at Crackers. "It was the parrot!"

"Parrots repeat what they hear," Captain Corky explained. "Someone must have taught him to say that."

"I think I know who," George said, eyeing Poppy.

"That was fun!" Poppy exclaimed as she ran over. "I want to play a game now. How about hide-and-seek?"

"Yeah, you hide—and stay there," Damien grumbled.

"Come on, yer lily-livered, blabbin' bird," Captain Corky said, picking up Crackers. "Back on the boat!"

While the captain carried Crackers to the boat, Casey suggested another game, called Blindfold Water Balloons.

The kids giggled as they covered their eyes with colorful bandannas. Nancy felt something squishy being stuck into her hands. It felt like a big fat water balloon!

"Throw the balloons back and forth without getting wet!" Casey's voice said. "Ready, set . . . pirates ahoy!!"

Water balloons began flying from hand to hand. Between giggles Nancy heard music in the distance. She quickly forgot about the tune when a water balloon burst cold water down her leg. After the last balloon burst, the kids lifted their blindfolds. Everyone laughed at how wet they all were—everyone but Poppy.

"Where'd Poppy go now?" Ivy asked.

Poppy was nowhere on the beach. But Nancy did spot Casey walking up the dock to the boat. He seemed to be dragging something shaped like a picnic cooler.

"Why would Casey leave his own game?" Nancy asked Bess and George. "And what's inside that cooler?"

"Maybe food from the party," George said. "Pirates have haaaargh-ty appetites, you know."

"Avast me hearties!" Captain Corky shouted as he walked over. "There's treasure thar on Teasdale Beach. But only the boldest buccaneers can find it."

Mrs. Fayne explained the game. Ivy and Damien would be the treasure hunters. Nancy, Bess, and George would be their first mates, giving them clues along the way.

"Clues are our business," Bess told the twins. "We're detectives, you know."

Nancy gave the first clue: "My hair is reddish, my eyes are blue. Leaves and twigs are the first clue!"

Ivy and Damien ran toward a tree, not the bushes.

"Don't do the math," George hinted next. "Just look near the path."

The twins searched the area near the path. They were warmer but not hot.

"My turn!" Bess declared. "My clue is totally bodacious. Go and look under the bushes."

"Bess!" George wailed as the twins ran off. "That wasn't a clue—you told them exactly where it was!"

"I didn't say *which* bush!" Bess insisted.

The girls caught up with the twins. Damien

was kneeling next to the bushes, his hand stretched underneath.

"There's nothing here," Damien reported.

"Huh?" Nancy said, surprised. "It has to be there."

"Let me look," George said. Dropping to her knees she practically crawled underneath the bushes.

"What do you see, George?" Nancy asked.

"Just dirt and a bunch of pebbles," George said. She looked up with wide eyes. "The treasure chest is *gone!*"

# ChaPTER ThREE

## Hide and Freak

"You mean we found the treasure?" Ivy asked.
"But we *didn't* find the treasure?"

"I don't get it!" Damien said.

"Neither do we," Nancy admitted. "It was there when Bess checked on it."

"For sure," Bess insisted.

"What was inside it?" Ivy asked.

"All sorts of neat pirate party favors," Nancy said, and sighed. "Eye patches, beads, telescopes—"

"Grandmaaaaaa!" Damien yelled into his cell phone. "Somebody stole our party favors!"

In a blink Mrs. Teasdale was on the beach, wearing sunglasses and a floppy hat. Mrs. Fayne raced over with Captain Corky at her side.

"Teasdale Beach is a private beach!" Mrs. Teasdale said after hearing about the missing treasure chest. "No one is allowed on it without my permission!"

"The path to Barnacle Beach is behind the bushes, Grandma," Ivy pointed out. "Anyone could have seen it."

"But we hid it very well," Nancy said.

"You should have buried it," Damien complained. "That's what you do with treasure chests."

"Buried treasure! Buried treasure! Raaak!"

Nancy turned to see Crackers perched on Casey's shoulder. Both had returned from the boat. Next to Casey stood Poppy, a big grin on her face.

*Why did I pick the bushes as a hiding place?* Nancy wondered. *What was I thinking?*

"Sorry, Mrs. Teasdale," Mrs. Fayne said. She forced a smile. "But there's still birthday cake for the kids."

"Cut pieces for your girls, then send the rest of the cake to the mansion," Mrs. Teasdale ordered. She raised an eyebrow. "Before *that* goes missing too."

Poppy snickered meanly. But Ivy turned to the girls and smiled.

"You said you're detectives, right?" Ivy asked. "So why don't you help find the missing treasure chest?"

Nancy's eyes lit up. What a great way to make up for her mistake.

"What do you think?" Nancy asked Bess and George.

"I think we should go for it!" George said.

"The Clue Crew is on the case," Bess declared.

"You mean the Clue-less Crew," Damien muttered.

"I heard that, Damien Teasdale," George said.

Captain Corky cleared his throat, then

24

declared, "Yo, ho, ho! A pirate's life is a busy life, so we'll be sailin' off now."

Nancy watched as Casey followed his father to the boat. Crackers was squawking like crazy. But Casey was as quiet as a mouse.

"Ivy, Damien, Poppy, let's go back to the house now," Mrs. Teasdale said. She nodded at Mrs. Fayne and the girls. "Thank you for your help . . . I think."

The Teasdales made their way to the mansion. All Mrs. Fayne could do was heave a big sigh and say, "Let's collect our things and get back to the hotel."

The girls watched quietly as Mrs. Fayne trudged back to the picnic table to pack up the cake.

"The treasure chest was there when I checked," Bess insisted. "Right before we played that water balloon game."

"Which means," Nancy said, thinking, "the treasure chest was stolen sometime during the water balloon game."

"But we were all playing that game," Bess said.

"Not all of us," Nancy disagreed. "When I pulled my blindfold off, Poppy wasn't there—and she knew where we hid the treasure chest."

"Poppy was also mad at her cousins for having better birthday parties than hers," George added.

"Then it was Poppy," Bess said. "Case closed."

*Case . . . case . . . case*, Nancy thought. She blinked hard as she suddenly remembered. *Casey!*

"Casey left the water balloon game too," Nancy said. "And he was lugging that thing that looked like a cooler."

"It could have been our treasure chest," George gasped. "But how did Casey know where we hid it?"

"The pirates worked on the party," Nancy said. "Maybe your mom told them about the treasure chest."

"No wonder Casey wanted us to play a game

with blindfolds," George said, narrowing her eyes. "So he could sneak away without us seeing a thing."

Bess raised her hand, jumped up and down, and said, "I remember something else. Damien told Casey he wouldn't be a real pirate unless he found a treasure chest."

"Then why didn't he tell us he found the treasure chest?" George wondered.

"Who knows?" Nancy admitted. "All I know is that we have two good suspects: Poppy and Casey!"

Nancy, Bess, and George searched for clues around the bushes. George spotted a Popsicle stick on the sand. There was no ice cream on it, just a bunch of red and brown ice-cream stains.

"Could be a clue," George said, reaching for it.

"Ewww, George!" Bess cried. "Don't pick up something that someone had in their mouth."

"We've had grosser clues than this," George said. "Like that nasty-looking toenail we found with the—"

"Don't remind me, please!" Bess cried.

George wrapped the Popsicle stick in a tissue and stuck it in her pocket. But as Nancy studied the many different footprints around the bushes she had a thought.

"Maybe more than one person took the treasure chest," Nancy said. She and her friends kneeled to examine the bushes. Bess found a strand of red hair wrapped around a twig.

"Ouch! Did that hurt, Nancy?" Bess asked.

"It's not my hair," Nancy answered. "My hair is reddish-blond. That hair is copper-penny-red."

"Now I know this case is getting hairy," George said. She tried to unwind the hair, but it was wound too tightly.

The girls helped Mrs. Fayne load the van. Then they headed back to Barnacle Betty's.

"I want to open up a case file on my mom's computer," George said as they entered the lobby. "Just like at home."

They were about to head to their room when

a woman's voice squealed, "We saw him! We saw him!"

Nancy, Bess, and George whirled around. A couple wearing bathing suits and cover-ups stood near Betty's desk. They waved their hands as they both spoke at once.

"There he was on the beach," the man boomed, "as green as the first day of spring!"

"Who? Who?" Nancy asked.

"Who else?" the woman asked. "Lonny the Lake Lizard!"

They couple showed the girls the pictures they took. Each one showed a human-size lizardy creature dragging his long tail across the sand.

"That's him?" Bess gulped.

"He was far away, but close enough to see it was Lonny," the man said excitedly.

"I told you folks you'd see Lonny the Lake Lizard," Betty said with a grin. "Now, aren't you glad you came?"

"You betcha!" the man said, pulling out his wallet. "I'll take a Lonny T-shirt—extra large."

"And I'll buy one of those cute Lonny caps," the woman piped up. "And a Lonny bobble-head doll."

"Bobble-head doll, coming up," Betty declared.

Bess waved Nancy and George away from the desk. "Didn't Betty say whatever Lonny wants, Lonny takes?" she whispered.

"Yeah, so?" George whispered.

"So maybe," Bess said, her eyes flashing bright, "the thief who took our treasure chest . . . is Lonny!"

# ChaPTER FOUR

## Upside Frown

"Why *can't* a lake monster be a suspect?" Bess asked later that day.

Nancy and her friends were sharing a giant pink raft shaped like a giant cell phone. It bobbed gently as it drifted on the lake.

"Because I don't believe in monsters!" Nancy insisted. She waved to Mrs. Fayne sitting on a towel on the beach.

The raft bounced as Bess turned toward George. "We saw the pictures, and seeing is believing—right, George?"

"Mmm-hmm," George mumbled. She was lying on her stomach with her eyes closed.

"Don't fall asleep, George," Bess said, shaking

her cousin. "If Lonny is our suspect, how do we question him?"

"Very carefully," George said, her eyes still closed.

Nancy sat up, making the raft bounce. "I want to question our other suspects, Poppy and Casey," she said. "At least we know they're human."

Mrs. Fayne waved for the girls to come in. Using their hands, Nancy, Bess, and George paddled the raft to the beach.

Carrying the raft over their heads, they walked past the lifeguard. The teenage boy sat straight in a high chair and stared out at the lake.

"Excuse me," Bess called up, "but did you ever see Lonny the Lake Lizard?"

"Hasn't everybody?" the lifeguard asked.

"See?" Bess whispered to Nancy and George. "He *is* real."

Back at the hotel the girls changed into dry clothes. The night air was cool, so they needed sweaters and hoodies.

"Mom? Can we go to the Teasdale house and say hi to Poppy?" George asked.

"Yes, but be quick," Mrs. Fayne said. "I have a surprise for you girls tonight."

"What is it?" Nancy asked excitedly.

"It wouldn't be a surprise if I told you, right?" Mrs. Fayne said with a grin.

At the Teasdale mansion Poppy was sitting on the doorstep, gently stroking a snowy white cat. The cat wore a pink jeweled collar.

"Hi, Poppy," Nancy said as they walked up the path.

When Poppy saw Nancy, Bess, and George, her eyes bugged out. The cat jumped off Poppy's lap as she stood up.

"Leave me alone!" Poppy told the girls.

Poppy charged into the house and slammed the door shut.

"You forgot your cat!" Nancy called.

Bess smiled at the cat on the doorstep. "Hi, pretty kitty," she cooed.

The cat arched her back and let out a loud *hisssssss*.

"Even their pets hate us," George said. "Let's get out of here."

The girls returned to the hotel, where they found out Mrs. Fayne's surprise: a trip to the Barnacle Beach fun park called Lonny Land.

After hamburgers and lemonade at a local diner, Mrs. Fayne drove the girls to Lonny Land. Nancy could see why they called it a fun park: It was filled with rides, games, and tons of people!

"I need to buy tickets for the rides," Mrs. Fayne said. "Stay here, stick together, and I'll be right back."

Music from the rides filled the air as the girls gazed around the park.

"What ride should we go on first?" Nancy asked. "The Bobbing Bobsled, the Trip to Pluto, or the Freaky Frog Hopper?"

"Whichever one doesn't go upside down," Bess said. "Did I tell you that I hate rides that go upside down?"

"Just about a million times," George groaned.

A bunch of kids walked by wearing bright green T-shirts. On the front of the shirts was a cartoony looking frog.

"What's the frog for?" Nancy asked.

"Maybe this town has a frog-monster, too," George said.

Nancy, Bess, and George watched a ride called the Loopy Lonny. It looked like an octopus with whirling arms. At the end of each arm was a cage. Kids inside the cages screamed as their cages flipped upside down.

"There's a handle inside each cage to flip it upside down!" George said excitedly. "It looks awesome!"

"You mean aw-ful!" Bess cried. "No way will I go on that."

As Nancy turned toward Bess she spotted the Teasdales—Mrs. Teasdale, Damien, Ivy . . . and *Poppy*!

"There she is!" Nancy hissed, pointing toward

the family. She and her friends crouched behind a peanut cart. They peeked out and watched as Mrs. Teasdale bought Loopy Lonny tickets for her grandchildren. Poppy dropped an empty peanut bag on the ground.

"Sloppy Poppy!" Bess whispered with a frown.

"If Poppy is going on the Loopy Lonny," Nancy whispered, "we should go on it too."

"Not me!" Bess hissed.

"Yes you!" George said. "We promised my mom we'd stick together, remember?"

The twins and Poppy ran to line up for the ride. Mrs. Teasdale plopped down wearily on a nearby bench.

"I have a few dollars to buy our own tickets," Nancy said. She and George flitted over to the ticket booth. Bess followed, complaining all the way.

"If I barf, it won't be my fault," Bess warned. "And upside-down barfs are the worst kind."

A ride attendant lifted the rope to let riders on. Poppy raced inside an empty cage. She waved to her brother and sister to join her. But Nancy, Bess, and George jumped inside the cage instead.

"You again?" Poppy wailed when she saw them. "I told you to leave me alone!"

The attendant fastened their safety harnesses. But the minute he slammed the cage door shut, Nancy demanded, "Where were you while we were playing the water balloon game, Poppy?"

The cage lifted off the ground. Soon the Loopy Lonny was whirling their cage around and around and around.

"I said, where were you during the water balloon game?" Nancy shouted over Bess's screams.

"None of your beeswax!" Poppy yelled back.

"That's it," George said. "You're going down!"

George grabbed the handle in the cage. She

gave it a yank, flip-flopping the cage upside down.

"Waaaaaaa!" Nancy and Bess shrieked. As they hung upside down like bats, something dropped out of Poppy's pocket. It landed on the upside-down ceiling with a *clunk*. As the cage

flip-flopped right side up, the object dropped into Nancy's lap.

Nancy glanced down and gasped. In her lap was a toy telescope—the same toy telescope that was in their treasure chest!

# ChaPTER FiVe

## Moonlight Fright

The Loopy Lonny kept whirling. But that didn't stop Nancy from firing questions at Poppy. "Where did you get this toy telescope, Poppy?" she shouted.

"At the store!" Poppy said. "I bought it myself!"

"How much did it cost?" George demanded.

"Um . . . um . . . twenty dollars?" Poppy squeaked.

"Twenty dollars for a plastic telescope?" George cried. "Now I know you're lying."

The ride finally slowed down. Bess swayed back and forth in her seat, her hand clapped over her mouth.

"Where is the treasure chest?" Nancy asked again.

"I didn't take the *whole* treasure chest," Poppy admitted. "I just took one thing from it!"

"The toy telescope?" Nancy asked.

Poppy nodded. Then she began to explain.

"Remember when I told you to look at Lonny on the lake?" Poppy asked. "When you turned around, I took a telescope. I really wanted beads, but that was on top."

The ride stopped, and the cage doors snapped open. After the harnesses were unbuckled, the riders stepped out.

"No wonder they named it after Lonny," Bess groaned miserably. "I must be green by now too."

Ivy and Damien were waiting at the gate for Poppy. But Nancy still had more questions for their little cousin. . . .

"You left the water balloon game the same time the treasure chest was stolen," Nancy said. "Where did you go?"

"To get ice cream!" Poppy answered. "I heard the Captain Creamy truck, so I took off my blindfold and ran!"

"Why did you want ice cream when there was food at the party?" George asked.

"Du-uh!" Poppy said. "Nothing is yummier than a Captain Creamy chocolate bar dipped in strawberry sauce!"

Nancy remembered hearing some kind of music during the game. Could it have been the Captain Creamy truck?

"Okay, now that I answered your questions," Poppy said, folding her arms, "can I have my telescope back?"

"No, way!" Nancy said. "You stole it."

"Then can I at least have the gum I stuck on the bottom of it?" Poppy asked. "I didn't finish chewing it!"

"Ew!" Nancy said, tossing the telescope back to Poppy.

The girls watched Poppy run over to Ivy and Damien.

"I tried to see if Poppy had chocolate or straw-berry stains on her shirt," Bess said. "But she was wearing a jacket."

"Chocolate and strawberry!" Nancy repeated. Then something clicked. "Just like the red and brown stains we found on that Popsicle stick!"

"Maybe the Popsicle stick belonged to Poppy," Bess said. "We saw her throw garbage on the ground before."

"Maybe," Nancy agreed. "But I still want more proof."

Mrs. Fayne hurried over with books of tickets. "Sorry, girls," she said. "The line for tickets was so long!"

"That's okay, Mom," George said. She glanced sideways at her friends. "We found something to do."

They were about to head for the bumper-car track when a jingly tune filled the air.

"Do you hear that?" Nancy asked.

"It's probably from one of the rides," George said.

"I don't think so," Nancy said. She listened closer. Then she got it. "That's the same music I heard during the water balloon game!"

With Mrs. Fayne behind them, the girls followed the sound to the park gate. Looking out they saw a truck parked on the street. It had a giant spinning ice-cream cone on the roof and the words CAPTAIN CREAMY painted on the side.

"Poppy said she bought ice cream from Captain Creamy when the treasure chest went missing," Nancy said. "So if I heard the Captain Creamy truck, she's probably telling the truth."

"So Poppy is clean," Bess said.

"Clean?" George scoffed. "That's a stretch!"

After bumper cars, carnival games, and a ride on the carousel it was time to return to Barnacle Betty's.

The lake sparkled under a full moon as the girls relaxed on the hotel's back porch. George sat crosslegged on the floor, typing on her mom's computer. Nancy and Bess played with a stuffed Lonny doll George won for knocking down bottles with a softball.

"How's the case file coming along?" Nancy asked.

"I'm up to our suspect list," George said as she typed. "Our only suspect left is Casey the kid pirate."

"No, he isn't. You're forgetting someone," Bess said in a singsong voice. She raised an eyebrow as she held up the stuffed Lonny doll.

"Lonny?" Nancy cried. "I told you, Bess, I won't believe in lake monsters until I see one with my own eyes."

"We have one day left," George said. "We have to question Casey first thing in the morning."

"But we don't know where he lives," Bess said.

Voices suddenly rose from the beach. By the light of the moon the girls saw people setting up chairs. Some were unpacking cameras and binoculars. One man was shining a super-bright flashlight at the lake.

"Why are they on the beach at night?" Nancy asked.

Before Bess or George could answer, a voice cried out, "There he is! There he is!"

More people began shouting in different languages. The only word Nancy understood was "Lonny!"

The girls leaned over the porch banister. Cameras flashed as a shadowy figure rose slowly from the water.

"Wow!" George gasped.

Nancy was too stunned to speak. The creature looked half-human, half-lizard, with a creepy fish-face!

The beach erupted in cheers as the giant lizard disappeared under the water: "Lon-ny! Lon-ny! Lon-ny!"

"*Now* do you believe in monsters, Nancy?" Bess asked.

Nancy gulped. If seeing was believing, then maybe she did!

# Chapter Six

## Trouble in Store

"I don't get it!" Nancy said the next morning. "Even if there is a lake monster here, why would he want to steal stuff like toy telescopes?"

"The better to see us humans, my dear!" George joked in a deep voice. "Mwah, hah, hah!"

"Quit it, George," Bess said, giving her a light whack. "Now I don't want to go in the water. I don't care how hot it gets."

The three friends sat in a red vinyl diner booth finishing breakfast. Mrs. Fayne was paying the bill at the cash register.

Sitting in the next booth were tourists from Japan. They had said hello to them during breakfast. Now they were looking at pictures they had taken of Lonny the night before. One man wore an I SAW LONNY T-shirt.

"I'm surprised this town doesn't serve Lonny Burgers," George muttered.

"They do," Bess said, pointing to the menu. "With bacon and cheddar cheese."

Mrs. Fayne returned to the booth. As she dropped her wallet into her bag she said, "You girls can help me run an errand this morning."

The girls exchanged worried looks. How could they run errands when they had to find Casey?

"What's the errand, Mom?" George asked.

"I want to visit a party shop called Chuckles," Mrs. Fayne explained. "And buy some balloons for my next party in River Heights."

"Does Chuckles just sell party stuff?" Bess asked.

"No," Mrs. Fayne replied. "I heard that Chuckles is famous for its costumes, too."

*Costumes, huh?* Nancy thought.

As they left the diner, Nancy whispered, "Do

you think that Lonny creature we saw was someone wearing a costume?"

"He looked pretty real to me," Bess said. "But some costumes look real too."

"If Chuckles sells lake lizard costumes," George said, her eyes wide, "that could prove Lonny is a fake!"

Chuckles was two blocks from the diner, on a busy street called Wharf Way. They were about to walk inside when Nancy saw a girl walking with her mother. She was wearing the green froggy T-shirt they had seen at Lonny Land. She also had bright copper-penny-red hair.

"Bess, George," Nancy said, "that girl's hair is the same color as the hair we found!"

"Lots of kids have red hair," George said. "Even you."

"My hair is reddish-blond," Nancy said.

"Close enough," George said sighing.

As the girls followed Mrs. Fayne into the store, they could see why it was called Chuckles. Hanging from the ceiling were rubber chickens and all kinds of funny hats. A glass case was filled with fake fangs, mustaches, rubber lips, and whoopee cushions!

"Girls, this is Lou," Mrs. Fayne said. "He's owned this store for about thirty years!"

A gray-haired man stepped over and grunted. Nancy gasped when she saw his nose. It was enormous and covered with huge warts!

"What are you looking at?" Lou asked. "Do I have spinach in my teeth?"

"Um . . . your nose," Nancy blurted.

"I have spinach in my nose?" Lou demanded.

"No!" Nancy said. "It's . . . it's . . ."

"It's fake!" Lou said. He plucked the nose off his face. "We're having a sale on rubber and plastic noses. Three for a dollar. Three-fifty for pig snouts."

The girls giggled as Lou popped the nose back on his face.

"Do you also sell costumes that look like Lonny?" Nancy asked. "You know . . . fish-face . . . scales . . . buggy eyes—"

"Lonny costumes?" Lou cut in. "There's only one Lonny in this town. And he's as real as the nose on my face."

Lou left to help Mrs. Fayne find balloons.

"Lou's nose is fake," Nancy whispered.

"So?" George asked.

"So if Lonny is as real as the nose on his face—Lonny is fake too!" Nancy explained.

The girls explored Chuckles. Behind shelves stocked with animal masks, giant clown feet, and colorful wigs was a door. A sign on the door read COSTUMES.

"Maybe the Lonny costume is in there!" Nancy whispered. She pulled open the door, and the girls slipped inside. Beside racks of costumes were metal shelves stacked with boxes and clear jars.

"Ew! Rubber eyeballs!" Bess said, pointing to a jar.

"Forget the eyeballs, Bess," George said. "Just keep your own eyes peeled for that Lonny costume."

The girls rummaged through three racks of costumes. They found a bunny costume, a tiger costume—even a costume that looked like a soup can. But no Lonny the Lake Lizard costume!

"Where else could it be?" Nancy asked. She looked around the room and saw another door. Curious, she grabbed the doorknob and pulled gently. The door swung open and—"Eeeee!!" Nancy screamed under her breath.

Something green and scaly with a creepy fish-face sprung out. It landed on Nancy, knocking her to the floor.

"It's him," Bess squeaked. "It's Lonny the Lake Monster!"

# CHAPTER SEVEN

## Treasure Pest

Nancy didn't want Lou to hear her scream. So her scream came out muffled: "Get it off me!"

George pulled the heavy rubber costume off Nancy. As Nancy stood up, she lifted the tail. Hanging from it was a tag that read LOU, MEND THE RIP IN THE TAIL.

"See, Bess?" Nancy said. "It's just a costume."

"I knew that," Bess said, her voice cracking.

Nancy studied the costume. Lonny was a fake, but what if he was still a thief?

"What if the person in the costume stole our treasure chest?" Nancy wondered. "He's always on the beach, right?"

"Right, but how do we find out who's wearing the costume?" George asked.

"We use this," Bess said. She walked over holding a jar in her hands. Packed inside the jar was white powder.

"What's that?" Nancy asked.

"I'll bet it's fingerprint powder!" Bess said excitedly. She began unscrewing the lid. "We can dust the Lonny costume for fingerprints like the TV detectives do!"

George read the label on the jar. "That's not fingerprint powder, Bess," she said. "It's—"

"Ahh-choooo!" Bess sneezed.

"Sneezing powder," George finished.

"And now you got sneezing powder all over the Lonny suit," Nancy pointed out. "We'd better wipe it off!"

They were about to do so when Mrs. Fayne's voice called, "Girls? Where are you? I'm ready to leave!"

They quickly shoved the Lonny costume and head back inside the closet. All three friends were sneezing as they darted out of the back room.

"Where were you?" Mrs. Fayne asked, holding a plastic Chuckles shopping bag.

"Um . . . we were looking for sneezing powder," Nancy said. "And we . . . ah-chooo!"

"We found it," Bess sniffed.

"The sneezing powder's in the back room," Lou said, almost to himself. "How did you—?"

"Well, we certainly don't need any of that stuff!" Mrs. Fayne cut in. "Come on, girls, time to go."

Nancy saw Lou eyeing them as they left the shop. Did he know they were in the back room? Did he know they found the Lonny costume?

The girls lagged behind Mrs. Fayne as they made their way back to the hotel.

"Lou acted funny when we asked him about the Lonny costume," Nancy pointed out.

"Maybe Lou's the person inside the Lonny costume," Bess said. "Do you think he also stole our treasure chest?"

"Why would he want our party favors?" George asked.

"So he could sell them in his store," Nancy figured. "If only we could go back and look for sparkly eye patches, beads, telescopes—"

"Raaaak!"

Nancy gasped as something feathery landed on her shoulder. She turned her head and smiled. It was Captain Corky's parrot Crackers!

"Avast, me hearties! Arrrk!" Crackers screeched.

"Where did you come from, Crackers?" Nancy asked.

The parrot didn't answer. But the girls did see a house off the path—a house flying a pirate flag in the front yard. Under the white skull and crossbones were the words CORKY THE PARTY PIRATE!

"That's probably where Casey lives!" George

exclaimed. "Now we can question him."

"Good boy, Crackers!" Nancy said with a smile.

"Good boy, good boy, arrrk!" Crackers screeched.

The girls ran up to Mrs. Fayne. She smiled when she saw Crackers.

"We want to bring Crackers back to his house, Mom," George said. "And say hi to Casey while we're at it."

"What if no one is home?" Mrs. Fayne asked.

"There's Crackers's perch," Bess said. She pointed to a wooden perch set up on the porch. "We can leave him there."

"Okay," Mrs. Fayne said. "The hotel is just around the corner. Stick together and come back in an hour."

"Thanks, Mom," George said.

"Thanks, Mom! Thanks, Mom! Raaaak!" Crackers screeched. He flew straight to his perch while the girls walked up a pebbly path. Half-way to the house Nancy noticed a fresh mound of dirt in the front yard. Sticking out of the dirt was a tiny flag. It was just a piece of paper stuck to a pencil with the words X MARKS THE SPOT!

"Something is buried there," Nancy said.

"Buried treasure! Buried treasure! Arrrrk!" Crackers screeched from his perch.

"Our missing treasure chest!" George exclaimed.

The girls fell to their knees and began digging with their hands.

"My nails are getting dirty," Bess complained.

"Wait!" George said. She ran to grab a small metal shovel leaning against a tree. "This will do the trick."

Nancy and Bess stepped back as George dug. After a while the shovel hit something hard, with a—*CLUNK!*

"We found it!" Nancy cheered. She brushed the dirt aside. Underneath was something that looked like a lid.

Nancy grabbed the lid and pulled. As it popped open, so did her eyes. Inside were no sparkly eye patches, beads, or toy telescopes. Just hundreds of red plastic coins!

"Looks like we found treasure," Bess said.

"Yeah," Nancy said. She scooped up a handful of fake coins. "But the wrong treasure chest."

# ChaPTER EighT

## Sign in the Sand

Nancy, Bess, and George tried to lift the treasure chest out of the ground.

"It's heavy!" Bess grunted.

George fell back on the ground as she yanked out the treasure chest. Before they could open it a voice shouted:

"Avast bilge-sucking landlubbers!"

Nancy looked up to see Casey jumping down from a tree. He was dressed in the same pirate gear he had worn to the party.

"Think ye can rob a pirate of his treas— aaaargh?" Casey shouted as he waved a floppy balloon sword. "Prepare ye for doom, lily-livered scoundrels!"

Nancy, Bess, and George stood up.

"Take a chill pill, bucko," George said. "We were just looking for our missing treasure chest." She pointed to the coins inside the chest. "Where did that come from?"

"I'm not telling you!" Casey sneered.

"I knew it." George sighed. "You're just a party pirate. If you were a *real* pirate you would have found buried treasure—"

"I did find buried treasure!" Casey blurted. "I found that chest on Barnacle Beach during the party!"

Nancy smiled at George. Good thinking!

Casey then pulled a piece of paper from his pocket. He unfolded it and held it up. "See?" he said. "I even found a treasure map that led me to it!"

Nancy, Bess, and George leaned over to study the map. It showed an arrow snaking past Teasdale Beach to Barnacle Beach, and an X that marked the spot.

"Where did you find the map, Casey?" Nancy asked.

"The wind blew it over while we were playing that water balloon game," Casey explained. "You didn't see it because you had blindfolds on."

"So you followed the map?" Bess asked.

"What else would a pirate do?" Casey said. "The map led straight to a lump of sand near the lifeguard's chair. I kicked away the sand until I found the treasure chest!"

"I don't get it," George said. "If you found buried treasure, why didn't you show it to anybody?"

"I was going to, after the party," Casey said. "But when your treasure chest went missing, I changed my mind."

"Why?" Nancy asked.

"I was scared you'd want my treasure chest instead," Casey explained. "So I kept my mouth shut."

The girls took a few steps back from Casey.

"It could still be our treasure chest," Bess whispered. "Casey could have taken out our party favors and filled it with those plastic coins."

But George shook her head.

"I helped Mom pick out the treasure chest for the party," George said. "Ours was black. That one is brown."

Nancy had enough proof. She was pretty sure Casey was innocent.

"Sorry we blamed you, Casey," Nancy said. "We were just doing our job."

"What job?" Casey asked.

"We're detectives," Nancy explained.

"Cool!" Casey exclaimed. He handed Nancy the treasure map and one red plastic coin. "Then you might need this as, what you detectives call, evidence!"

"Thanks," Nancy said.

"Fair winds, mateys!" Casey declared. He gave a little wave and scurried back up the tree.

Nancy glanced up to see a tree house shaped like a shipwreck. "I'm glad Casey didn't steal our treasure chest," she said. "He is kind of nice."

"In a weird kind of way," George added.

"Casey weird! Casey weird!" Crackers squawked from his perch. "Raaaak!"

Casey glared down from his tree house and shouted, "I heard that, scalawags!"

The girls hurried away from Casey's house.

"Do you think the stuff he gave you are clues?" George asked Nancy.

"Probably not," Nancy said with a smile. "But they're neat souvenirs from our trip to Barnacle Beach."

After eating sandwiches at the hotel, it was time for the beach. Mrs. Fayne lounged on a striped beach chair, reading a book. Nancy, Bess, and George shared a bright blue beach towel on the sand.

Under the hot summer sun Bess slathered on more coconut sunscreen. George was updating their case file on the computer. Nancy was busy talking to her father on Mrs. Fayne's cell phone. . . .

"Our only suspect is some person in a lake monster suit, Daddy!" Nancy told him. "And our best clue is a red hair we found at the scene of the crime."

Mr. Drew worked as a lawyer, so he was an

expert when it came to working on cases. He helped Nancy and the Clue Crew whenever he could.

"You know, clues are a bit like treasure chests," Nancy's father said.

"Treasure chests?" Nancy said, wrinkling her nose. "What do you mean, Daddy?"

"In order to find them," Mr. Drew explained, "you have to keep digging."

Nancy giggled, then said, "Then we'd better start digging fast, Daddy. We're going home tomorrow."

"I know!" Mr. Drew said. "Hannah is already baking your favorite veggie lasagna."

"Mmm!" Nancy said. She could practically smell her housekeeper's lasagna over the phone. But Hannah was more than the Drews' housekeeper. Ever since Nancy's mother died when she was three years old, Hannah had cared for and loved Nancy just like a real mother would.

"See you tomorrow, beach bunny," Mr. Drew said.

"See you, Daddy," Nancy said. After blowing a ton of kisses over the phone, she clicked it off.

"Dad says to keep digging for clues," Nancy remarked.

"Okey-doke," Bess said. She was flipping the red plastic coin Casey had given them in her hand.

"Why are you carrying that thing around, Bess?" George asked.

"Because it could be a good-luck coin," Bess said. "And with this case, we can use all the luck we can get."

Bess looked at the coin closely. "Hey," she said. "It's got a frog design on it. Are frogs good luck?"

Nancy looked too. The coin did have a frog on it. She wondered why, until a voice interrupted her thoughts. . . .

"Hey, Clue Crew!"

Nancy turned to see Ivy and Damien walking over. Damien was wearing a light blue polo shirt and khaki shorts. Ivy had on a white sundress. Both were wearing identical rubber sandals.

"What are you doing hanging on the beach?" Damien asked. "Shouldn't you be looking for our treasure chest?"

"We're always looking," George said. "Even when we're not looking!"

"We even have a new suspect," Bess said with a smile. "Lonny the Lake Monster."

The twins' jaws both dropped. Nancy was about to explain that it wasn't really Lonny— but it was too late!

"Lonny?" Ivy cried.

"Now I know you're not real detectives," Damien groaned. "You think a giant lizard stole our party favors."

The twins began walking away. Nancy, Bess, and George stood up to run after them. But the sand was too hot under their bare feet.

"Ouch!" Bess said as they jumped on a grassy patch.

"They think we're looking for the real Lonny," George groaned. "No wonder they think we're nuts."

Nancy didn't really care what the twins thought of them. She only wanted to solve the case, once and for all.

"If Lou from Chuckles is inside that Lonny suit, we have to catch him in the act," Nancy said.

"There's not enough time." Bess sighed. "We're leaving Barnacle Beach tomorrow morning."

"There's enough time for a stakeout," George suggested. "We can hide on the beach until we see Lonny."

"What do we do when we see him?" Nancy asked.

"We pull off his mask and call him a fake," George exclaimed. "Whether it's Lou, or some other sneaky guy."

"Who says we need a stakeout?" Bess said.

She pointed to the sand. "Lonny is closer than we think!"

Nancy and George looked to see where Bess was pointing. There on the sand were footprints—giant lizardy footprints!

"Where did they come from?" George asked.

"There's only one way to find out," Nancy said. "We have to follow those footprints."

Nancy returned Mrs. Fayne's cell phone. Then the girls tracked the footprints back to Barnacle Betty's hotel.

"The footprints start at the cellar door," Nancy said. "Whoever's in the costume must have climbed out of the cellar."

The girls followed the footprints. They ended at a giant rock on the beach.

"Where'd he go?" George wondered.

Suddenly the person in the Lonny suit darted out from behind the rock. As he ran toward the lake, Nancy yelled, "Stop! We know you're in there!"

"Step out of that costume!" George shouted. "I repeat—step out of that costume!"

Lonny froze. He began turning slowly toward the girls.

"Okay," George murmured, her voice shaky. "Who's going to pull off the mask?"

"I'm not tall enough," Bess said. "Or brave enough!"

Nancy was losing her courage too. "You guys"—she gulped—"what if that thing isn't a costume? What if it really *is* a monster?"

# CHAPTER NINE

## Ah-Choo Clue

"I'm not waiting around to find out," George said, turning to run. "Let's get out of here."

Nancy was about to run too, until Lonny threw back his enormous head and let out a huge—"Ahh-choooo!"

"Do we say 'gesundheit'?" George whispered.

The girls watched as Lonny sneezed over and over again. Then somewhere between an "ah" and a "choo," something clicked . . .

"There *is* a person inside that costume," Nancy said.

"How do you know?" Bess asked.

"Remember how you got sneezing powder all over the Lonny suit?" Nancy asked with a smile.

Two big clawed hands reached up to remove the Lonny mask. When Nancy saw the face underneath, she gasped. It wasn't Lou or a guest at the hotel. It was—

"Barnacle Betty!" Nancy cried.

"Ahhhhh-choooooo!" Betty sneezed. The sneeze was so powerful, she raised the sand around her giant rubber feet.

Betty sniffled and said, "Cheese and crackers! I never sneezed like that in my life!"

"Sneezing powder," Bess said. "My bad."

Remembering the girls, Betty scooted back behind the rock. The girls ran behind it too.

"So you were Lonny all this time!" Nancy said.

"Now you know my secret," Betty said.

"Lou called to say you girls were onto something. But I never thought you'd figure out that Lonny wasn't real."

"We didn't figure everything out," Nancy admitted. "Like, why did you dress up like Lonny in the first place?"

"I did it for tourism!" Betty declared.

"Tourism?" George repeated.

"People come from all over to see Lonny," Betty explained. "I have to give them their money's worth."

Betty waved her free arm as she went on. "This whole town was built on Lonny the Lake Monster. Captain Creamy even named an ice cream after him!"

"Is it green?" Bess wanted to know.

But Nancy wanted to know something else.

"Speaking of Captain Creamy," Nancy said. "Where were you yesterday when his truck stopped near the beach?"

"Captain Creamy usually comes around in

the early afternoon," Betty said. "I was at my desk then."

"How do you know?" George asked.

"I was checking in a tour from Japan," Betty said. "I'll show you my check-in book if you'd like."

Nancy remembered the Japanese tourists. And since Betty offered to show them her check-in book, she must be telling the truth.

"Oh, phooey," Betty said, and sighed. "I suppose you girls are going to tell the whole world my little secret."

Nancy shook her head. "We don't want to spoil all the fun, Betty," she said.

"Your secret is safe with us!" George promised.

"Good!" Betty said with relief. "Because I'm paying a visit to Camp Bumpy Bullfrog next week—as Lonny!"

"There's a camp here?" Bess asked.

"A day camp," Betty explained. "Practically

all the kids at Barnacle Beach go to Camp Bumpy Bullfrog."

Betty pulled the mask over her head.

"I'd better take this costume to Lou's to be cleaned," Betty said, "before I sneeze my *real* head off."

The girls could hear Betty sneezing as she trudged across the beach as Lonny. People on the beach squealed and pointed to her. One of them was Mrs. Fayne!

"Oh, great," George groaned. "Now I have to keep a secret from my mom."

But Nancy's mind wasn't on Lonny anymore. It was on Camp Bumpy Bullfrog.

"There were frogs on those green T-shirts we saw," Nancy said. "Maybe the kids wearing them were Bumpy Bullfrog campers."

"There was a frog on the plastic coin, too," Bess remembered. "The one from Casey's treasure chest."

"What does Camp Bumpy Bullfrog have to do with our missing treasure chest?" George asked.

Nancy tapped her chin thoughtfully. Then she said, "What if the treasure chest Casey found belonged to the Bumpy Bullfrog campers? And the chest the campers have is ours?"

"Let's check out the treasure map Casey gave us," Bess said. "I packed that in my beach bag too."

The girls raced back to their beach blanket. Bess pulled out the treasure map, and they studied it carefully.

"The arrow leads past Teasdale Beach to Barnacle Beach," Nancy pointed out. "It goes right past the bushes."

"They might have seen our treasure chest on the way," George said.

Nancy glanced at her waterproof watch. "Camp is probably over for the day," she said. "But first thing tomorrow morning we'll get hopping."

"Was that a bullfrog joke?" Bess giggled.

"I guess." Nancy giggled too. But she was totally serious about finding their treasure chest once and for all.

❀ ❀ ❀

"We're leaving Barnacle Beach today, girls," Mrs. Fayne said the next morning. "There's no time to work on your case."

The girls stood around their suitcases in the lobby of Barnacle Betty's. They were all packed and *not* ready to go!

"Can't you bring us to Camp Bumpy Bullfrog on our way home?" George pleaded.

"Please?" Nancy asked.

"With sugar on top?" Bess added.

Mrs. Fayne finally agreed. "But only for half an hour," she said. "Then it's back to River Heights."

After a good-bye to Betty, Nancy, Bess, and George helped load the van. They climbed into the backseat and buckled their seat belts. While Mrs. Fayne looked for her car keys Nancy saw Ivy and Damien watching from the road.

"Are you going home without finding our treasure chest?" Damien called.

Bess stuck her head out of the window and

shouted, "We think some kids at a camp know where it is!"

"If our treasure chest is in some camp, I want to get it myself," Damien insisted.

"Me too!" Ivy said.

The twins climbed into the back of the van. Poppy ran to the side of the road just as they slammed the door shut.

"You two can't come without telling your grandmother first," Mrs. Fayne told Ivy and Damien.

"Okay, I'll have Poppy let her know," Ivy said. She rolled down the window and yelled out, "Tell Grandma we went with Mrs. Fayne, Poppy!"

"I want to go too," Poppy yelled as the van took off. "It's not fair! It's not fair!"

Camp Bumpy Bullfrog was about a mile away from Barnacle Betty's. But a sign forbid Mrs. Fayne from driving onto the campgrounds.

"You kids go inside," Mrs. Fayne said. "But come back soon so I can drive Ivy and Damien home."

The kids ran through the gate into the camp. They walked past a tennis court, swimming pool, even a miniature golf course. Kids in green T-shirts were busy having fun.

"Why didn't Grandma tell us about camp?" Ivy asked.

Nancy looked around. Where would they begin to look for the treasure chest? But as they passed the rec hall she saw a sign over the door.

"'Treasure Hunt Party,'" Nancy read aloud.

The kids peered through the windows. Nancy saw a pirate flag hanging on a wall and black balloons hanging from the rafters.

"Look," Bess said. "On the table!"

Nancy pressed her nose against the glass until she spotted the table. On it was a black and white tablecloth and—

"Our treasure chest!" Nancy gasped.

# CHAPTER TEN

## Hop, Hop, Hooray!

"We have to go in there," Nancy said. She pulled at the door, but it was locked.

"See you guys inside," Damien said. He hoisted himself up and climbed through an open window.

"He can't break in like that!" Nancy cried.

"We have to get him out of there," Ivy said.

One by one the girls climbed through the open window. Inside, Damien was reaching for the treasure chest.

"Stop, Damien!" Nancy shouted. "Breaking in is wrong!"

"What do you think *you* guys just did?" Damien asked.

The girls traded embarrassed looks.

"Whoops," Bess said.

"Okay, since we're in here already," George said, "let's check out the treasure chest."

Damien pulled open the lid. He looked inside and said, "Phooey."

The girls ran to look inside the chest too.

"It's empty," Nancy groaned.

"Where are our party favors?" Ivy demanded.

"I don't know," Bess said. She pointed to the snacks on the table. "But those cookies look yummi-licious!"

Bess was about to grab a cookie when Nancy heard voices outside: "Yo, ho, ho, ho, ho!" they chanted.

"Someone's coming," Nancy whispered.

George fell on her knees and began crawling under the table. "Come on," she hissed. "Hide under here!"

The others crawled under too. The tablecloth covered them like a tent.

"I feel like I'm camping!" Bess said.

"Shh!" Nancy whispered. "If they find us, we're toast!"

"You mean toasted marshmallows," George whispered. "This is camp, remember?"

Nancy lifted the tablecloth and peeked out. The door was just swinging open. A teenage girl wearing a pirate hat stepped inside. Filing in behind her were kids dressed as pirates too. They wore sparkly eye patches and beaded necklaces. One boy pressed his eye to a toy telescope, pointed it toward the table, and declared, "Avast, me hearties! Grub ahoy!"

"They have our party favors," Nancy whispered.

Suddenly Bess let out a piercing shriek. A big, fat frog was jumping back and forth underneath the table. Ivy screamed too, as it hopped into her lap. She flicked the frog to Nancy, who didn't mean to catch it—but she did!

"Ew!" Nancy cried, tossing the frog out from under the table.

"It's Hopalong!" a girl cried.

Nancy held her breath as someone lifted the tablecloth. A boy wearing a yellow bandanna on his head peered underneath the table and said, "Who are these guys?"

"Busted," Damien groaned.

Nancy and the others crawled out from under the table.

"Thanks for finding Hopalong," a girl replied. "He's our camp mascot."

Nancy stared at the girl. She was the same girl they saw yesterday—the one with the copper-penny-red hair!

"Hopalong went missing a few days ago," the girl said, holding the blurping, kicking bullfrog.

"So did our party favors," Damien said, pointing to the chest on the table. "And we want them back."

"No way!" the red-haired girl said. "I got my hair tangled on a twig pulling that thing out."

*So that's how the hair got there,* Nancy thought.

Nancy was about to ask nicely for the treasure chest when the campers began chanting, "Finders, keepers, losers, weepers!"

The teenage girl raised her hands for quiet. She turned to Nancy, Bess, George, Damien, and Ivy and said, "I'm Lindsay, the counselor. What were you doing in our rec room? Don't you know it's wrong to break in?"

"Yes, and we're sorry," Nancy admitted. "We wanted to see what happened to the favors from the pirate party."

"Pirate party?" the bandanna-boy said. "You mean all this neat stuff came from that party we were invited to?"

"You guys were invited?" Damien asked with surprise.

"Why didn't you come?" Ivy asked, surprised too.

"We wanted to," a girl with green sneakers said. "But we all had camp that day."

"I planned a treasure hunt instead," Lindsay explained. "But I guess the kids found the wrong treasure."

"A better one!" a boy with dark curly hair said. "It had neat pirate stuff. Ours just had stinky fake coins!"

Deep inside, Nancy was cartwheel-happy. The Clue Crew had solved the case in the nick of time. Now all they had to do was get the party favors back to the twins.

"Look, you guys," Nancy told the campers. "Can't you please—"

*WHAM!* She stopped mid-sentence as the door

flew open, slamming into the wall. Nancy's eyes popped wide open as Mrs. Teasdale and Poppy raced in.

"There they are, Grandma!" Poppy said, pointing her finger at Ivy and Damien. "They left without telling you!"

"Ivy, Damien!" Mrs. Teasdale scolded. "I'm very disappointed in you!"

"Sorry, Grandma," Ivy said. "But so are we—in *you*."

"What?" Mrs. Teasdale gasped.

"Why didn't you tell us these kids couldn't come to our party because they had camp?" Damien asked. "We thought they didn't *want* to come."

"And why didn't you tell us about Camp Bumpy Bullfrog, Grandma?" Ivy asked. "This place looks neat!"

Mrs. Teasdale shuffled her feet and cleared her throat. Finally she shrugged and said, "I suppose I was afraid to tell you about camp."

"Afraid?" Ivy and Damien said together.

"I wanted you to spend time with me—not at camp all day!" Mrs. Teasdale exclaimed. "I'm so lonely in that big house—even with Fluffernutter."

"Fluffernutter?" Nancy whispered.

"Must be that hissy cat," George whispered back.

Nancy pictured the Teasdale mansion inside her head. It was way-big. But way-big houses meant way-big parties!

"I know how you can fill up that house fast, Mrs. Teasdale," Nancy said with a smile. "Why don't you invite the kids of Camp Bumpy Bullfrog for a beach barbecue?"

"A beach barbecue," Mrs. Teasdale said slowly. "I haven't had one of those in years!"

"You can have it on a Saturday," Bess suggested, "so the Bumpy Bullfrog campers can come."

Mrs. Teasdale's eyes twinkled, and she clapped her hands. "We can have a clambake," she said. "And play beach blanket bingo."

Ivy, Damien, and the campers cheered.

Nancy, Bess, and George exchanged high fives. But Poppy just scowled.

"What about our treasure chest?" Poppy demanded.

"Oh, yeah," Damien said. Then he gave his hand a wave. "Ah, let those guys keep it."

"Sure," Ivy said, nodding. "They're coming to our beach party. They might as well keep the party *favors*."

George suddenly remembered her mom waiting in the van. After a quick good-bye, the girls raced out of the rec room. As they made their way through Camp Bumpy Bullfrog they talked about the case. And they had plenty to talk about!

"Not only did we find the treasure chest," Nancy said, "we found a ton of new friends for Ivy, Damien, and Poppy!"

"Speaking of Poppy," George said, nodding over her shoulder. "Look who's right behind us!"

Nancy turned to see Poppy. She was racing after them with a big smile on her face. But this time it was a nice smile, not a mean one.

"You guys gave me an awesome idea for my next birthday party," Poppy said. "And it won't be at Chucky Chicken."

"What is it?" Bess asked.

"A mystery party!" Poppy exclaimed. "Do you think you can come?"

The girls traded smiles. Nancy turned to Poppy and said, "Sure. There are two things the Clue Crew can never get enough of."

"What?" Poppy asked.

"Friends," Nancy answered. "And *mysteries*!"

# Beach in a Jar

What's the best thing about a day at the beach? Splashing in the waves, building sand castles, and collecting shells. What's the worst thing? Having to leave after all that fun!

No worries. Now there's a way to take a bit of the beach home with you. It's easier than you think and totally beachy-keen!

## You Will Need:

Clear glass jar with wide lid (try a mayo jar)

Glass cleaner

Paint and brush

Sand

Shells, pebbles, gull feathers, small pieces of driftwood—or any other tiny treasures you found on the beach

Craft glue

# How to Assemble Your Own Private Beach:

❀ Unscrew lid and place aside.

❀ Use glass cleaner to remove smudges and fingerprints inside and outside the jar.

❀ Stand jar on its bottom or side.

❀ Pour sand into the jar (enough to cover the bottom).

❀ Place or drop shells and other items inside the jar (use a spoon to carefully scoop objects onto the sand).

❀ Paint the lid of the jar a fun color and let it dry.

❀ Glue a bigger shell, feather, starfish, or other beachy item on top of the lid.

❀ After the glue dries, twist the lid tightly to close the jar.

❀ ❀ ❀

(For extra fun, decorate your beach with mini paper umbrellas, silk butterflies, or doll accessories like tiny sunglasses or sandals. Fill your room with beach music to set the mood. Ask your mom or dad about the Beach Boys!)

Most of all, have fun making your own beach in a jar. It's the next best thing to the *shore* thing!

Turn the page for a sneak peek at

# Nancy Drew

## AND THE CLUE CREW

 **#21** Double Take

"Last one dressed is a rotten egg!" someone shouted. A wave of girls ran into the locker room, screaming and laughing.

"No running!" the gym teacher, Mr. Wilson, called out. "Everyone, please walk!"

Nancy, Bess, George, and all the other girls slowed down as they squeezed through the doorway. Gym class was over, and it was the end of the day. They had had fun playing dodgeball outside in the warm sun. Now it was time to get changed and go home.

Inside the locker room, all the girls rushed to their lockers. Things were kind of a mess, though. There were clothes strewn all over the floor from before class, when everyone had been in a huge hurry to get changed for gym.

Nancy stepped over a pile of skirts, jeans, and T-shirts and walked over to locker #9. She remembered that she was using locker #9 today because the number 9 was the same as the month of September. She opened her locker; her jeans and purple top were hanging neatly on hooks, and her backpack and shoes were lined up at the bottom. She was glad her things weren't all over the floor, like some of the other girls'.

Nancy started to change, then noticed that Nadine was changing a couple of lockers over. Nancy gave her a small wave. "Are you still mad at Antonio for what he did at lunch?" she called out.

Nadine nodded, her eyes blazing. "He almost ruined my Lula Rappaport hoodie! I'll never, ever forgive him!" she said dramatically. Nadine wanted to be an actress when she grew up, so she was always saying things in a theatrical way.

As if on queue, a girl with long, curly red hair walked up to Nadine and tapped her on the shoulder. Nancy recognized her. It was Violet Keeler, a new girl in their class.

"Hey, Nadine? I heard through the grapevine that you have the new Lula Rappaport hoodie," Violet said eagerly. "I don't know if you know this, but I'm the world's biggest Lula fan. In fact, check out this T-shirt. I made it myself."

Violet unzipped her sweatshirt to reveal a white T-shirt. The words LULA ROCKS had been stenciled across the front of it, in pink.

"That's a cool T-shirt," Nancy said.

"Definitely," Nadine agreed. She sat down on a bench and pulled on a pair of yellow polka-dot socks.

Violet tapped Nadine on the shoulder again. "Hey, Nadine? I was wondering. Could I *buy* your Lula hoodie from you? I looked for it everywhere, but I can't find it. I'll give you my life's savings for it. I have $21.58. No, $21.59. *Plus* I have a twenty-five dollar savings bond that my grandparents gave me. You can cash it in for $25 in like five years."

Nadine shrugged apologetically. "Thanks, but I can't sell my hoodie. It was a present from my aunt Chloe, and it's like my favorite piece of clothing that I own."

Violet looked disappointed. She thought for a moment. "Then could I just kind of borrow it? For my birthday party, which is going to have a really, really awesome Lula theme? It's in three weeks, and if you let me borrow it, I would totally invite you and make you the guest of honor and everything."

Nadine shook her head. "No, I don't think so." She added, "But I check out clothes websites a lot. I'll let you know if I see the Lula hoodie somewhere."

Violet frowned. "Oh . . . okay. I guess," she mumbled. She sounded disappointed.

Nancy watched as Violet took off. She had no idea that Violet was such a big Lula Rappaport fan!

"Let's go to my house," Nancy suggested.

"No, let's go to *my* house," Bess said. "My mom baked toffee brownies yesterday. Yum!"

"No, let's go to *my* house," George said. "I want to show you guys this cool new computer game I got. It's called Revenge of the Beastly Bunnies!"

The three of them were standing in front of the school, trying to decide whose house to go to. The air was crisp, and the leaves were just starting to turn gold and red. Nearby, some kids were getting on the bus. Some kids were being picked up by their parents or their sitters. And some kids, like them, were getting ready to walk home by themselves. Nancy was allowed to walk to and from school without grown-ups, since it was less than five blocks from her house.

"Maybe we should flip a coin," Bess suggested. "Except we would need a three-sided coin to decide between our three houses!" She giggled.

Just then, Nadine came rushing up to them. Her face was flushed, and she looked upset.

"Nadine, what's the matter?" Nancy asked her.

"I have the most awful, horrible news in the world!" Nadine burst out. "My Lula Rappaport hoodie is missing!"